IN THE BIG INNING
BIBLE RIDDLES
FROM THE
BACK PEW

written by Mike Thaler   illustrated by Jared Lee

YUMMY!

ZONDERkidz

ZONDERVAN.com/
AUTHORTRACKER
follow your favorite authors

What is God's favorite snack food?

Praisens.

To Patty Thaler
My bride, my wife, my life
—M.T.

To cousin, Roselyn Poulson
—J.L.

ZONDERKIDZ

In The Big Inning
Copyright © 2010 by Mike Thaler
Illustrations © 2010 by Jared Lee Studio, Inc.

Requests for information should be addressed to:

Zondervan, *Grand Rapids, Michigan 49530*

Library of Congress Cataloging-in-Publication Data

Thaler, Mike, 1936–
    Bible riddles from the back pew / by Mike Thaler; illustrated by Jared Lee.
        p.   cm. – (Tales from the back pew)
        ISBN 978-0-310-71597-9 (softcover)
    1. Riddles, Juvenile. 2. Bible—Juvenile humor. I. Lee, Jared D., ill. II. Title.
  PN6371.5.T46 20010
  818'.5402—dc22
                                                  2009007394

Editor: Mary Hassinger
Art direction: Merit Kathan

Printed in China

10 11 12 13 14 /LPC/ 6 5 4 3 2

What kinds of tea does God like best?

Purity and humility.

What tea takes forever to drink?

Eternity.

How do we get away from sin?

We take it on the lamb.

Why did Satan tempt Eve with an apple?

Because he was rotten to the core.

How do you know Adam and Eve played board games?

Because they had a paradise.

How do you know Adam and Eve were good at math?

Because God told them to multiply.

How do you know Adam became a sinner?

Because he was Abel to raise a little Cain.

What job did God pick Noah for?

To be his "ark-itect."

Which one of Noah's sons became an actor?

Ham.

How do you know they played tennis in the Bible?

Because the Bible tells us that Joseph served in Pharaoh's court.

Why did the ruler of Egypt make the Israelites slaves?

Because he was unfair-oah.

Who were the two shortest guys in the Bible?

Knee-high-miah and Bildad, the Shoe-height.

Where did Isaiah get the prophesy of Jesus' birth?

He looked at Immanuel.

What kingdom in the Bible made the best sandwiches?

Ba-baloney-a.

WOW!

What monster did the three wise men bring to baby Jesus?

The Bible says they brought gold, Frankenstein, and myrrh.

Who was the first Irishman mentioned in the Bible?

Nick O'Demis.

How do you know Jesus traveled with two oxen?

It says he taught with pair-a-bulls.

Where do you get filled with the Holy Spirit?

At a pul-pit stop.

FILL'ER UP, PREACHER.

AMEN.

GAS

What do you call a pure sermon?

Pastor-ized.

MILK →

Why do Christians shine?

Because they're filled with Son-light.

What is God's greatest gift to us?

His presence.

I will now put forth a riddle unto you.
—Judges 14:12